Daphne Moves to Hawai'i

Written by Alison Berka

Iillustrated by Susan Brandt

MUTUAL PUBLISHING

ISBN 1-56647-702-6
Library of Congress Catalog Card Number: 2004112033

Design by Jane Hopkins

First Printing, November 2004
1 2 3 4 5 6 7 8 9

Mutual Publishing, LLC
1215 Center Street, Suite 210
Honolulu, Hawai'i 96816
Ph: (808) 732-1709
Fax: (808) 734-4094
e-mail: mutual@mutualpublishing.com
www.mutualpublishing.com

Printed in Korea

To Mike, Max, Rachel and Sam

Mahalo for your love and support

— A.B.

Daphne had a great life. She lived in a cozy warm house with her friend Pork Chop, the bulldog, and the Wimbly family. Megan Wimbly took wonderful care of Daphne and Pork Chop. She gave them sausage treats. She played chase in the backyard with them. She dressed them up in exotic costumes and danced with them.

One day, Daphne noticed a change in the cozy warm house. The Wimblys were putting everything into cardboard boxes. Mrs. Wimbly kept biting her nails. Mr. Wimbly was busy taking things off shelves and out of closets.

By the end of the day, the cozy warm house was empty and Daphne was put into a plastic box with mesh windows instead of her bed. Soon Daphne settled down and fell asleep.

After a long time, someone opened the door to her plastic box. Daphne yawned and poked her head out. She saw the Wimblys smiling at her. They were in a cool breezy house with a lot of open windows.

"Aloha, Daphne, my little wahine," said Megan putting a ring of flowers around Daphne's neck. "Welcome to Hawai'i!"

Daphne looked around. Where was the cozy warm house?

Megan unpacked Daphne's favorite food dish and filled the bowl with sausage treats. Daphne turned up her nose.

Megan dug in a box and pulled out Daphne's "Dozy Doo Doggie Bed" covered with fuzzy fake fur. Daphne looked at it in a daze.

Megan put a tiny aloha shirt on Daphne. She felt strange in the silky fabric. Pork Chop just yawned and went to sleep in a corner.

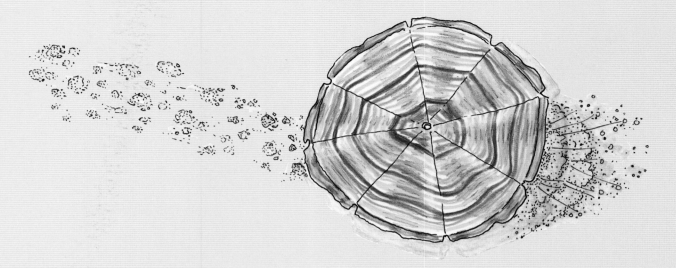

The next morning the Wimblys went to the beach. Megan rolled down the car window so Daphne could stick her head out. Instead, Daphne put her head on the seat. She wished she could curl up by the kitchen window in the cozy warm house and go to sleep. Maybe this was all a bad dream and if she took another nap she would wake up back home.

At the beach Daphne could barely walk in the soft sand. It was so hot it burned her paws. Pork Chop lumbered over to the umbrella, dug a little trench, and settled in the shade.

"I don't like it here," Daphne said to Pork Chop. "I miss the cozy warm house with the grass yard." Pork Chop snorted and burrowed further into the sand.

Daphne watched Megan run to the water. It rushed in at her and then rushed back out. She screamed and laughed, playing chase with the water.

"Why is she playing chase with the water instead of me?" thought Daphne.

Everything was different.

Daphne wanted everything to be normal again. She needed to find the cozy warm house. Without looking back, Daphne ran to the road while the Wimblys were swimming. She looked both ways, but didn't know which way led to the cozy warm house.

There by the side of the road sat a fat, brown bufo frog.

"Hello," Daphne said.

"Aloha, my little furry friend. You must be new in town," the bufo said with a thunderous burp.

"Yes, I am. And I'm looking for the way back to the cozy warm house," Daphne said.

"Cozy house?" The bufo slowly looked to the right and slowly looked to the left. "Only cozy houses I know are the bungalows at the Coconut Niu Hotel. Just follow the signs with pictures of coconuts on them. Good Luck!" He winked with one of his large round eyes. Then he hopped away and disappeared under a bush.

Daphne wondered what a coconut was. Maybe it was something like the hot cocoa Megan would sip on cold winter days.

Daphne continued up the road looking for signs with pictures of hot cocoa on them.

Soon she saw a mongoose.

"Hi there," Daphne said.

The mongoose stopped and looked at Daphne, "Aloha! I didn't see you. I was busy trying to cross the road. It's very important to look both ways on a highway before you run across. You never know when a car or a truck might come, and if you aren't careful…oh my, you'll end up flatter than a surfboard," she said wringing her paws. "Can I help you get across?"

"I don't know," said Daphne. "I'm looking for the signs with pictures of hot cocoa that will lead me to the cozy warm house."

"I don't know of any hot cocoa around here. Maybe you'll find some at Banana Bob's. He makes an 'ono banana smoothie. Follow the road until you come to an intersection. Turn in the direction of the gnarly old mango tree. You can't miss it. Oh look, the road's all clear. Hurry up now, wikiwiki and be careful!" With a quick wave good-bye the mongoose bolted across the road.

Daphne wondered what a mango tree was. Mr. and Mrs. Wimbly sometimes put on snappy music and danced the tango. Maybe this was a dancing tree.

Daphne hurried up the road looking for an intersection with a dancing tree.

Soon she came upon a gecko sunning himself on a rock.

"Excuse me…" Daphne said to the gecko.

"Aloha, I am Gecko Extraordinaire, master of disguises, surprises and magical performances. May I be of service to you?" He adjusted his sunglasses and gave Daphne a welcoming smile.

"Yes, I was wondering if you know where I can find the tree that dances the tango? You see, I'm trying to find the place that makes banana smoothies that has the signs with pictures of hot cocoa that will lead me to the cozy warm house."

"Oh, well, let me see," said the gecko. "I'm afraid I don't really know how to tango. I do a fabulous hula though. Let me show you!" He jumped off the rock and began to dance.

"I learned this at Iwalani's Halau. It's the best hula school on the island. Maybe they know some tango dancers."

"How do I find Iwalani's Halau?" Daphne asked.

"You'll have to take the next left and follow the wall of lava rocks until you come to the place. Say 'aloha' to Iwalani for me. She's my favorite auntie. Gotta go. Too much sun is bad for the complexion. Aloha!" He waved at her with a friendly shaka and scampered over the rocks.

Daphne wondered what lava rocks were. Maybe they were like the java beans that Mr. Wimbly brought home for his breakfast coffee. Mr. Wimbly had stopped making coffee from them because they made him jumpy.

Daphne set out to find a wall of jumpy rocks.

Soon she came to a Hawaiian duck, or koloa, pecking at seedpods on the ground.

"Excuse me, but do you know where I might find the wall of jumpy rocks? I'm told they will lead me to the hula school that has the tango dancers who can show me the way to the dancing tree that will point me in the direction of the smoothie shop which will have signs with pictures of hot cocoa that will lead me to the cozy warm house," Daphne said hoping she hadn't forgotten anything.

"Oh dear, sit down right here and let me think. I'm afraid I don't know of any rocks that jump. I know rocks that fall, rocks that tumble, and of course, rocks that skip on water if thrown properly. But they don't jump around here. In fact, I've never seen a rock jump," she said looking sadly at Daphne. "Now if it's jumping you want, I would suggest getting a nice jump rope. I hear that Leilani the lei seller has some excellent jump ropes at her lei stand. She makes them out of beautiful plumeria flowers. Just go down the road and you'll see them on the fence in front of her stand. Oh dear, I better go. I have to babysit the keiki. Aloha!" And she waddled off.

Daphne wondered what a lei was. Megan always said, "Now I lay me down to sleep" before she went to bed. But the koloa said it was a lei stand, which didn't make any sense to Daphne. How could you lay yourself down and stand at the same time?

Daphne's head hurt, and she missed Megan.

Daphne trudged forward. She wasn't sure where she was going or what she was looking for. All she knew was that she wanted to be home where she could cuddle next to Megan and munch on sausage treats. She even missed the sound of Pork Chop snoring.

A light rain fell as Daphne walked. Soon the rain was coming down hard, soaking Daphne. It was getting dark and she desperately wanted to find the cozy warm house.

Up ahead a soft light glowed. As Daphne approached, she saw a small figure sitting on the lānai. Daphne dashed up the steps to the shelter of the house.

"Daphne!" cried Megan
as she swept the dripping dog
in her arms and hugged her
tight. "We've been looking for you."
Even Pork Chop let out a bark and
wagged his tail.

Daphne felt warm and snug. This was what
she had missed about the cozy warm house. It was Megan and her
parents, the smell of dinner cooking and playing with Pork Chop.
Everything was right here in Hawai'i.

Daphne ran over and grabbed an aloha shirt with her teeth and brought it to Megan. Megan put the aloha shirt on Daphne. Then she strummed her 'ukulele, and they all danced the hula in the cool, breezy new house.